THE
LION KING

Herds of animals had traveled far and wide across the Pride Lands to celebrate the birth of King Mufasa's son.

At the top of Pride Rock, Rafiki, the wise old baboon, approached King Mufasa and Queen Sarabi. He took Simba, their lion cub, to the edge of the rock and held him up for all to see.

Only one family member was missing from the ceremony: Mufasa's brother, Scar.

"I was first in line to the throne… before that little hairball was born," said Scar.

"That 'hairball' is my son, and your future king," Mufasa replied.

One morning, Mufasa brought Simba to Pride Rock and said, "Look, Simba. Everything the light touches is our kingdom, except the Shadowlands. That place is beyond our borders, and you must never go there."

Simba couldn't resist showing his father how brave he was.
He ran to find his best friend, Nala. As they played, they got closer
and closer to the Shadowlands until, suddenly, they stumbled across
an enormous skull.

At that moment, three laughing hyenas encircled them. Simba and Nala were scared. The hungry hyenas chased the cubs until they cornered Simba. They were about to attack when…

… a big paw swiped down at the hyenas, sending them flying. The hyenas landed in a pile of bones. Mufasa had come to their rescue!

"Never go near my son again!" he roared. The hyenas were no match for Mufasa, and they scampered away.

Ashamed, Simba approached his father.

"I was just trying to be brave like you," he said sheepishly.

Mufasa couldn't help but smile. "Being brave doesn't mean you go looking for trouble."

At that same moment, Scar was striking a deal with the hyenas. He promised them that they could live on the Pride Lands if they killed Simba and Mufasa.

The next day, Scar led Simba to a deep gorge. On Scar's orders, the hyenas sent a pack of wildebeest stampeding towards Simba! Nearby, Mufasa could see a cloud of dust rising from the gorge and went to investigate.

When he saw that his son was in trouble, Mufasa didn't hesitate.
He jumped into the gorge to save Simba from the stampeding herd.
He carried the cub to safety before being swept away by the wildebeests.
When the herd had passed, Simba went in search of his father.
When he found him, Mufasa was dead.

Just then, Scar emerged from the dust.

"Simba, what have you done? The King is dead and it's all your fault! Run away and never return!" Scar told Simba.

Heartbroken and confused, Simba ran away as fast as he could.
He traveled through the scorching desert, injured and exhausted.
He walked as far as he could until he collapsed in a heap on the ground.

When he awoke, a warthog and a meerkat were hovering over him.

"My name is Timon and this is Pumbaa," said the meerkat, pointing to the warthog. "Listen to us: forget about the past and you'll have no worries! Hakuna Matata!"

Simba's new friends invited him to live with them, and Simba quickly adopted their way of life. He learned to eat insects, swim in the river, and play all day.

One day, Simba heard his friends' cries for help. Timon was trying to protect Pumbaa from a hungry lioness. Simba pounced!

The lions fought until the lioness pinned Simba to the ground. They looked at each other intently.

"Nala? It's me, Simba!" said the young lion.

"Simba! You're alive! We thought you were dead!" cried Nala.

Simba and Nala took a long walk through the jungle together.
Nala explained that Scar and the hyenas had ruined the Pride Lands.
She asked him to come back and help them, but Simba refused. He felt
responsible for his father's death and knew that he could never go back.

That night, as he gazed up at the stars, Simba met Rafiki. The wise old baboon recognized Simba as Mufasa's son and led him to a pond. He asked him to look into the water. Simba, who had expected to see his father, was disappointed to see his own reflection staring back at him.

"Your father lives in you," said Rafiki.

At that moment, Simba heard a familiar voice calling his name. He looked up to see Mufasa's face in the heavens.

"You are more than you have become. You must take your place in the circle of life. Remember who you are. You are my son, and the one true king," Mufasa told him.

Simba decided to return to the Pride Lands. When he reached the kingdom, he saw nothing but ruin and desolation. The herds had disappeared and all the plants had dried up.

As Scar was scolding Simba's mother Sarabi, a big lion appeared in a halo of light. It was Simba.

"I've come to take back my throne, Scar," he said.

Scar laughed. He signaled the hyenas, who surrounded Simba.

Scar and the hyenas led Simba to the edge of a cliff.

"Now this looks familiar," said Scar. "This is just the way your father looked before he died…"

After all these years, Simba finally discovered the truth.
Scar had caused his father's death! Simba climbed back up the cliff.
Now face-to-face with Simba, Scar panicked, and blamed the
hyenas for Mufasa's death. Simba let Scar go, but the angry hyenas
weren't so forgiving, and quickly encircled Scar. Simba let out a
victorious roar.

It wasn't long before the animals once again gathered to celebrate a royal birth. Simba and Nala watched proudly as Rafiki brought their cub to the edge of Pride Rock, and held her up for all to see.